A Synagogue Just Like Home

Alice Blumenthal McGinty   illustrated

CANDLEWICK PRESS

Rabbi Ruben treasured his synagogue—
from its cheery red bricks to its lively
windows to the musty, dusty attic up on
top. Each day there felt bright and new.

But his synagogue was not so new.

The sink in its huge,
homey kitchen leaked.

The floors in its wise
wooden library creaked.

And its sunny sanctuary had such drafts that at last
Friday evening's service, the Shabbat candles flickered
once, flickered twice, and then blew out!

Rabbi Ruben had to make things right. "Our synagogue should feel cared for, like a happy home!" he said.

So on Friday morning, he decided to fix things up as a
Shabbat gift for his busy congregation. First, he walked
into the sunny sanctuary.

"Hello!" he said to Mrs. Tuchclapper and the choir, who
were busy practicing for the service that evening. "You
sound awesome. Sing! Sing! Pretend I'm not even here."

Rabbi Ruben ran his hands along the nippy windows. Cold air streamed in everywhere. He knew what to do. He rolled up some old tablecloths and snugged them tightly around the windows.

"Perfect!" he said with a smile. "Warm and cozy, just like home. Now our Shabbat candles will burn bright!"

Next, he stepped into the wise wooden library.

Creak! went the floors. Ms. Havis looked up from studying the Torah.

"Just doing some fixing," Rabbi Ruben said, tiptoeing around Ms. Havis. "I'll be quiet as a deli on Yom Kippur."

He slid a hammer from the toolbox, then
pounded—*BANG, BANG, BANG*—on the creaky
floorboards until they sat a little straighter.
"Splendid!" said Rabbi Ruben.

Last, he went into the huge, homey kitchen, where Mr. Litwak and his helpers were baking challah and cookies for after the service.

"Don't mind me," Rabbi Ruben told them. "I'm not even here. Just fixing things for Shabbat."

He took a wrench from the toolbox and tugged, tugged on the faucet of the leaky sink.

But the leak didn't stop. It grew from a drip to a flow.

"Um . . ." said Mr. Litwak.

"No worries," Rabbi Ruben said. "This synagogue needs our care, like a wise old home!" He tugged again with the wrench. But the flow became a spurt.

"Ech!" said the rabbi.

"Would you like some help?" Miss Berger asked.

"Thanks, but no. I know what to do," said Rabbi Ruben, wiping water from his face.

He grabbed a pinch of challah dough from a rising loaf and pushed it into the leaky faucet . . . then a bit more, until it stopped. "No more leak!" he announced.

The synagogue was ready.

That evening, the congregation came together in the
sanctuary to welcome Shabbat as the sun went down.

The candles only flickered twice.

However, after the service, one of the Weinstein girls giggled and asked, "Why are there tablecloths in the windows?"

Rabbi Ruben blushed. "I was trying to stop the drafts," he mumbled.

"Ah." Mrs. Tuchclapper peeked in. "We just fixed our own drafty windows. The Tuchclapper clan can help."

"Can we help, too?" asked the Weinstein girls.

Rabbi Ruben grinned. "Of course," he said. "A home is about helping! And our synagogue is just like home."

Next, everyone went to the wise wooden library to return their prayer books. As they walked across the creaky floor, though, a board popped right under Rabbi Ruben's feet!

Rabbi Ruben gasped. "Oy, oy, oy! I thought I'd fixed the floor!"

Beside him, Ms. Havis sighed. "I've been wondering about those creaky old boards."

Several people agreed: "Time for a new floor."

"We're a team," Ms. Havis said. "We'll share the work and get it done."

Rabbi Ruben felt a wave of relief sweep over him. "A home is about sharing," he said.

Finally, everyone walked to the eating area to share Shabbat challah. Certainly, all would be well now, Rabbi Ruben thought.

Mr. Litwak and his helpers brought out the challah, tiny cups of wine, and platters of cookies. Then, preparing to lead the blessings over the wine and challah, the rabbi saw something shiny on the floor. "I left my glasses in the library," he said, squinting. "It must be a reflection."

But as the room quieted
and he lifted his wineglass
for the blessing, a yelp came
from near the kitchen,
followed by a wave of water.

"Ech!" the rabbi cried,
spilling his wine.

In the chaos, the rabbi ran into the kitchen. He
stared helplessly at the water spurting from the sink.
"Oy, what a mess," he moaned. "I've made our
synagogue cold and wet!"

Somebody placed a hand on his shoulder. Soon everyone surrounded him while Miss Berger turned off the water under the kitchen sink.

Rabbi Ruben looked down at the soaked floor. "I'd hoped to fix things, as a Shabbat gift. But I've ruined everything."

"Nonsense," Mrs. Litwak said. "Nothing is ruined. And we're here to help!"

"A home is about helping," the Weinstein girls said.

"A home is about sharing," said Ms. Havis.

"And a home is about caring," said the Tuchclapper boys.

"Caring for each other," added the littlest Litwak.

Rabbi Ruben grinned.

They worked all week long, the Litwaks cleaning carpets . . .
the Tuchclapper clan and the Weinstein girls sealing windows in
the sanctuary . . . Ms. Havis and her team laying a brand-new floor
in the library . . . Miss Berger fixing the kitchen sink . . . and all the
children polishing floors with mops and rags that Rabbi Ruben
found in the musty, dusty attic.

That Friday evening, when Rabbi Ruben lit
the candles in the sanctuary for Shabbat services,
they burned bright and strong.

He looked out at his congregation over the glowing flames, and his heart swelled. "Perfect!" he said. There they were, together—helping, sharing, caring.

And their synagogue felt just like home.

Glossary

challah (HAH-lah): special bread, often braided, eaten on Shabbat

sanctuary (SANK-choo-AIR-ee): the holiest part of the synagogue, where the altar is housed and where people pray

Shabbat (SHAH-baht or shah-BAHT): the Sabbath, or day of rest, celebrated each week from sundown on Friday evening until sundown on Saturday evening

Shabbat candles (SHAH-baht KAN-dulz or shah-BAHT KAN-dulz): two candles lit on Friday evening to usher in the Sabbath

synagogue (SIN-uh-gog): a Jewish house of worship

Torah (TOR-uh): the first five books of the Hebrew Bible, written on scrolls and read from each week on Shabbat

To the Havis family, whose home is
about helping, sharing, and caring
ABM

Text copyright © 2022 by Alice B. McGinty
Illustrations copyright © 2022 by Laurel Molk

First edition 2022
This edition published specially for PJ Library®/
The Harold Grinspoon Foundation 2022 by Candlewick Press

Library of Congress Catalog Card Number 2021948374

ISBN 978-1-5362-1086-6 (Candlewick trade edition)
ISBN 978-1-5362-2962-2 (PJ Library® edition)

22 APS 1

Printed in Humen, Dongguan, China

This book was typeset in Playfair Display and Bodoni 72 Oldstyle.
The illustrations were done in mixed media, finished digitally.

Candlewick Press
99 Dover Street
Somerville, Massachusetts 02144

www.candlewick.com

0922/B1899/A5

A JUNIOR LIBRARY GUILD SELECTION